Boyds will Be Boyds™

BEWARE of MAD DOG!

ISBN 0-439-57469-2

Text copyright © 2004 by Sarah Weeks.
Illustrations copyright © 2004 by Scholastic Inc.
All rights reserved. Published by Scholastic Inc.
SCHOLASTIC, Boyds Will Be Boyds, and associated logos are trademarks
and/or registered trademarks of Scholastic Inc.

12 11 10 9 8 7 6 5 4 3 2 1   4 5 6 7 8 9/0

Printed in the U.S.A.   40
First printing, February 2004

Boyds will Be Boyds™

BEWARE OF MAD DOG!

by Sarah Weeks

AN
APPLE
PAPERBACK

SCHOLASTIC INC.

New York Toronto London Auckland Sydney
Mexico City New Delhi Hong Kong Buenos Aires

CHAPTER ONE

"Come on, Nat, A or B?"

"It's not fair, you made it too hard, Fink. Give me a different one," I begged.

We were in the yard at school, waiting for the morning bell to ring, playing "A or B?", a game we invented together a long time ago. The way it works is one person has to think up two disgusting things, and then the other person has to choose which one he would rather do. You don't actually have to do the things in real life, you just have to say which one you would rather do if you had to do one.

"You know the rules," Fink said, "You *have* to choose one."

"Okay, fine. Give them to me again," I said.

"A: You hold hands with Marla Dundee in the lunchroom in front of everybody for five whole minutes, or B: You tell Jessie Kornblume you think she's hot."

I shook my head.

"No way. Just thinking about those girls makes me want to hurl. You have to give me another choice."

"Okay, fine. C: You eat a can of worms," he said.

"Live ones?" I asked.

"Live and lively," he said with a grin as he wiggled his fingers in my face.

"That's a no-brainer. Pass the worms," I said, and we both laughed.

Just then, Marla and Jessie walked by and gave us dirty looks. Jessie wears glasses and Marla doesn't, but other than that it's scary how much they're alike. They're both short and have curly red hair, freckles and beady little eyes, which they squinch up in a mean way whenever they look at us. That's because they can't stand us and, trust me, the feeling is mutual. WAY mutual. Fink did the worm fingers again, then poked me in the ribs so that I lost my balance and stepped on Marla's foot by accident.

"Ow! Ow! Ow!" she said, hopping around on her good foot. "I'm warning you, Nathaniel Boyd, if you broke my foot, my father's going to sue you."

Marla's father, Mr. Dundee, is one of those hot-shot lawyers who wears fancy suits and has a cell phone that's so small it's practically invisible. I see him out walking their dog all the time, always on his phone, usually yelling at the top of his lungs about nailing somebody to the wall. Whenever anybody crosses Marla or ticks her off, the first thing she does is threaten that her dad is going to sue them. I barely even stepped on her foot, but she was making a big deal out of it as usual.

"Sorry, Marla," I said. "It was an accident."

"Good thing feet come in pairs, so at least you've got a spare if Nat actually busted that one," Fink added.

Marla stopped hopping and squinched up her eyes at us even tighter than usual.

"Boys are so immature," she said.

"And *Boyds* are even worse," said Jessie. Then she pushed her glasses up the way she always does when she thinks she's said something clever.

"How unoriginal can you get?" asked Fink.

Fink and I have the same name. Only it's his first name and my last. I'm Nathaniel Boyd and he's Boyd Fink. It's a pretty unusual coincidence, and we think it's kind of cool, but we've been best friends since first grade, so believe me, we've heard all the jokes. And that wasn't even a very good one.

"Let's get out of here, Marla, before their lack of intelligence rubs off on us and makes us dumb like them," said Jessie as she took Marla by the arm, and the two of them walked away, their annoying red ponytails swinging together in perfect time.

Jessie Kornblume, who we call Corn Bloomers, got a 99.9 on the Farnsworth Aptitude test in third grade, and ever since then, she thinks she's some kind of genius and the rest of us are all morons. She's smart all right, but if you ask me, she's living proof that you can be smart and an idiot at the same time.

"Like I said, I'll take the worms any day," I told

Fink, as the morning bell rang and we all headed inside.

The best part of fifth grade is that Fink and I are in the same class. The worst part is that not only are Jessie and Marla in our class but so is Douglas Ditmeyer, better known as Mad Dog. I'm not afraid of heights, or spiders, or scary movies, but Mad Dog is a different story. I've done my very best to hide it. Fink is the only one I've ever actually admitted it to, but Mad Dog Ditmeyer scares the pants right off me.

Mad Dog is evil. Mad Dog is bad. Even back in kindergarten when we were all just a bunch of babies, he was rotten. He'd sneak into the closet and steal the Fruit Roll-Ups out of your lunchbox, or grab your pencil away and bite off the eraser. One time, he swiped a mousetrap with a dead mouse in it from the custodian's cart, and stuffed it in somebody's gym shoe. He got suspended for that, but when he came back, he was just as bad as before; he was just sneakier about it. Sneaky and evil is a very dangerous combo, in case you didn't know.

Our teacher is Mrs. West. She's sort of grumpy

and old, at least fifty, I'd say, and she doesn't hear very well, which is actually okay because sometimes when we talk during class, she doesn't notice. Not like Miss Haven, my fourth-grade teacher. She wasn't human. She heard sounds only dogs are supposed to be able to hear, and she could also tell if you had gum even when it was stuck to the roof of your mouth and you weren't chewing it AT ALL.

"We're starting our unit on exploration this week, and you'll be working in groups of four on your presentations," Mrs. West told us.

Fink's hand shot up in the air.

"Let me guess, Mr. Fink, you'd like to know if you can work with Mr. Boyd, is that correct?"

Fink nodded. Other hands went up, too.

"Just a moment, ladies and gentlemen. Hands down, please. I'm well aware that you would all like to work in groups with your friends, but I've taken the liberty of choosing the groups myself this time."

Everybody groaned. Jessie raised her hand politely.

"Yes, Miss Kornblume?"

Mrs. West always calls us "mister" and "miss" when she speaks to us.

"I don't think it's fair when you put one smart person in a group with three dumb ones," she said. "'Cause the smart one ends up doing all the work, and the dumb ones get a free ride."

"As you know, Miss Kornblume, I discourage the use of the word *dumb* in my classroom," Mrs. West said. "However, if the point you're trying to make is that you feel the workload should be shared equally among all four members of the group, I agree whole-heartedly."

Marla raised her hand.

"I prefer not to work with boys," she said. "They're too *immature*."

Ditmeyer slipped his hand under his shirt and made a rude noise with his armpit. When everyone laughed, Mrs. West whirled around, but by then, Mad Dog was sitting with his hands folded on his desk, looking innocent. At least, that's what I figured he was probably doing. I didn't actually look at him. I try not to since sometimes just making eye contact with Mad Dog is enough to set him off.

"That's enough," said Mrs. West sternly. "As I told you, the groups have already been chosen, so there's no need for further discussion. We'll start with group number one, which will be researching Ferdinand Magellan. Please listen for your names so I don't have to repeat myself."

I wasn't in the first group and neither was Fink, but Marla was. I breathed a sigh of relief; at least neither of us would have to put up with her. We weren't in the Amerigo Vespucci or Lewis and Clark groups either, but Fink's name was the first one called for group number four, Vasco da Gama. Mrs. West cleared her throat and called the second name — "Nathaniel Boyd."

Fink let out a happy *whoop*. I reached over and we high-fived.

"Man alive-o cool-o jive-o!" he said.

So far, so good. Fink and I were together. When Mrs. West called the next name, though, we both flinched. Jessie Kornblume was in our group. Ugh. That was definitely going to be a drag. At least we outnumbered her. Plus, she's smart and has good handwriting, which I figured would come in handy if we had to make any charts or maps. Fink and I are both really bad at that kind of junk.

I was so busy thinking about Jessie Kornblume's handwriting, I didn't notice that my right knee had begun to itch. But Fink saw me scratching, and he knew right away what was happening.

"Oh, no!" he gasped in horror. "The knee, Nat-man. The *knee*."

There's something you need to know about me, and I guess this is as good a time as any to tell you. I'm sort of, well, jinxed. No matter what I do or where I go, bad luck has a way of finding me and messing things up. It happens pretty often, and when it does, the only warning I get before it strikes is an itchy knee.

For a second I thought maybe the timing was off and it was leftover itching from when we found out we were going to have to work with Jessie, but that wasn't it. I had forgotten there was going to be one more person in our group. There were plenty of people left. We could have gotten Danny Lebson or Jenny Shaw or David Framer. Any of them would have been fine, but when Mrs. West called the name, I started scratching like crazy.

We got Mad Dog.

CHAPTER TWO

"I can't help it if I'm a bad-luck magnet," I said to Fink that afternoon at lunch.

"Maybe we should call you 'The Fridge,'" Fink said.

"What's that supposed to mean?" I asked.

"You know, refrigerators have all those magnets on them," he said. "Get it?"

"That's dumb," I told him.

"So's your thumb," he said.

"That's even dumber," I said.

"So's your plumber," he said.

"STOP!" I shouted. "Can't you see this is not

the right time to torture me with that annoying game?"

Fink made up this rhyming game he really loves to play. Every time I say the word *dumb*, he starts rhyming; and once we start, we don't stop until we run out of rhymes. I don't usually mind. In fact, sometimes it's pretty funny, but at the moment my mind was on other things.

"I was only trying to lighten things up a little," he said.

"There's no way to lighten this up. No matter how you look at it, it stinks," I said. "You know how I feel about Mad Dog."

"Yeah, Jessie Corn Bloomers AND Mad Dog. Talk about a double whammy," said Fink.

Just then, the Red Devils, our secret nickname for Jessie and Marla, walked over to us, holding their lunch trays in front of them.

"We've decided to lodge a complaint," Marla said.

"Huh?" said Fink.

"We're complaining," explained Marla, "to Mrs.

West. We want her to switch Jessie and I into the same group."

"Jessie and me," Jessie said, correcting Marla's grammar.

If Fink did obnoxious stuff like correct my grammar, I can guarantee you we wouldn't stay friends for very long, but Marla puts up with it for some reason. Probably because she's just as obnoxious. I'm sure she's threatened to sue Jessie, even though they're best friends.

"Yeah, it's only fair for us to get to work together since you guys get to," added Jessie.

"Great!" I said, thinking the most logical thing for Mrs. West to do would be to switch Marla with Mad Dog, so there'd be an even number of boys and girls in the group. As much as I disliked the idea of working with both Marla and Jessie, *anything* was better than Mad Dog.

A lot of good the complaining did. Mrs. West wouldn't change the groups. In fact, she got mad at Marla and Jessie for bugging her about it. I have to admit I enjoyed watching them get bawled out until I remembered that it meant Mad Dog was still going to be in the group with Fink and me.

Later that afternoon, I got a phone call.

"Honey, there's a girl on the phone for you!" my mother called up to my room.

No girl had called me since kindergarten, when I used to play with Pamela Welch because she had a very cool tree house in her backyard. Now Pamela is about ten feet tall and she looks really, well, different. I heard one of the parents saw her in the hall during open school week and thought she was a *teacher*. Anyway, like I said, Pamela hadn't called me since kindergarten, so I knew it wasn't her on the phone.

"Hello?" I said.

"It's Jessie. I'm calling to make a date," she said.

Holy smokes! Jessie Kornblume wanted to go out on a date with me. Had the world gone mad? Was life as I knew it coming to an end?

"Um, uh. What kind of date?" I stammered.

"What kind of date do you think, dumbo? A date to start working on our project," she said.

"Oh," I was so relieved. I felt faint and had to sit down.

"Can you come to my house tomorrow after school?" she asked.

"Tomorrow? I guess so. Will Fink be there, too?" I asked.

"Uh, duh. He's in our group, isn't he?" she said. "Do you always ask so many dumb questions?"

This was not going to be easy.

"Fine. I'll be there. 'Bye," I said, anxious to get off the phone as soon as possible.

"Not so fast!" she said. "I've decided you have to call Mad Dog and tell him about the meeting."

"Me? Why do I have to call him?" I said.

"I'm not making all the calls," she said. "It's not fair to expect me to do everything."

"Fine, we'll split the calls. You call Mad Dog and I'll call Fink," I said.

"I already called Fink; plus, I called you. That

makes two calls for me and none for you," she said. "Do the math."

My call-waiting beeped.

"Hang on," I grumbled.

It was Fink.

"Hey," he said. "You hear from Corn Bloomers yet? She left me a message about a meeting tomorrow."

"Yeah, she's on the other line right now. And guess what. She told me I have to call Mad Dog to tell him about the meeting," I said.

"You? Why can't she do it herself? I mean, it's at her house, isn't it?" he asked.

"Yeah, I know, but she says I have to because she already made two calls," I said.

"That's ridiculous. One call to Mad Dog is worth at least twenty calls to a normal person," Fink said. "Especially for you."

"So what do I tell her?" I asked.

"Tell her you're not going to do it and that's final," he said.

"Hang on," I said. "I'm going to tell her right now."

I clicked over to the other line.

"Jessie?" I said. "Since the meeting is at your house, you have to make all the calls."

"Oh, yeah? Says who?" she said.

"Says me, and that's final. I'm not calling Mad Dog," I said.

"Yes, you are. If you don't, I'll tell Mrs. West," she said.

"Hold on," I told her.

I clicked back over to Fink.

"Now she's threatening to tell on me," I said. "What should I do?"

"Threaten her back," he said.

I clicked back to Jessie.

"If you tell on me, I'm gonna tell on you, too," I said.

"Tell what on me?" she asked.

"I'll tell Mrs. West you're being bossy as usual," I said.

"Oh, yeah? Then I'll tell the whole class that you're afraid to call up silly old Douglas Ditmeyer on the phone. What a wimp!" she snorted.

"Hold on," I said.

I clicked over to Fink.

"She says she's going to tell the whole class I'm afraid of Mad Dog," I said.

Fink coughed and cleared his throat.

"*Are* you afraid of him?" he whispered.

"You know I am. More than anything," I said. "Just looking at him makes me sweat so bad I get B.O."

Fink started laughing this high-pitched, giggling kind of laugh that didn't sound anything like him.

"What's the matter with you, Fink?" I asked.

"*What's the matter with you, Fink?*" mimicked a mean voice.

It was Jessie! I must not have hit the flash button hard enough. I hadn't gone back to Fink at all. Instead I'd just told Jessie Kornblume that Mad Dog gave me B.O.!

"I didn't mean it," I said quickly. "I was only kidding."

"Oh, *really?* You mean you're not afraid of Mad Dog?" said Jessie.

18

"Of course not," I said. "Everybody knows his bark is worse than his bite."

I slapped my forehead in disgust. This was one of my mother's stupid expressions. They always seem to pop out at the worst possible time.

"Okay," Jessie said. "Since you say you're not afraid of him, I guess you won't have any problem calling him up then, *right*?"

"Of course not," I said, wishing I could fall through the floor and straight on through the other side of the earth to China.

"Tell him three-thirty at my house," said Jessie. "And Nat?"

"Yeah?" I said.

"Beware of Mad Dog. I don't know about barking, but I hear he bites." Then she giggled and hung up.

I was about to click back to Fink when I heard him calling my name as he came clomping up the stairs to my room. He only lives two doors away. I guess he got tired of waiting and decided to come over and see what was taking so long.

"What happened?" he asked.

I flung myself onto the bed. My knee was itching so badly I pulled up my pant leg and scratched at it furiously.

"What happened? Oh, nothing," I said. "Except that I just told Jessie Kornblume that Mad Dog Ditmeyer scares me so bad he gives me B.O."

"*What?* Why'd you do that?" said Fink.

"I didn't mean to. It was an accident. I thought I was talking to you, only it was really her because I didn't push the — oh, forget it. What difference does it make now? I'm doomed. Not only do I have to call Mad Dog, but now Jessie is going to tell that evil twin of hers what I said, and the two of them are going to torture me to death about it."

"Wow, no wonder you're scratching. I'm even a little itchy myself," Fink said, scratching his elbow.

"I'm doomed," I moaned again. "Totally doomed."

CHAPTER THREE

"Don't panic, Nat-o," said Fink. "The way I see it, you've got two problems here."

"You mean two disasters," I corrected.

"Whatever you want to call them, you've got two of them. Number one is that Jessie knows you're scared of Mad Dog now, right?"

"Right," I said.

"And number two is that you have to call Mad Dog today and tell him about the meeting," said Fink.

"Right," I said.

"Okay, let's deal with that one first, since it's easy," said Fink.

"It is?" I asked. The idea of picking up the phone

and calling someone I was terrified of didn't exactly fall under the category of "easy" as far as I was concerned.

"Sure. I'll just call Mad Dog for you," said Fink.

"Really?" I said. "You wouldn't mind doing that?"

"Nah," he said. "I don't like him, but it's not like he gives me B.O. or anything."

I shook my head.

"Why did I have to tell her that?" I groaned. "What an idiot I am!"

"Quit beating yourself up. Let's get this phone call over with, and then we can figure out a way to fix the thing with Jessie," said Fink. "Hand me the phone."

"Wait a second," I said. "Are you going to make the phone call as you or as me?"

"What do you mean?" asked Fink.

"If you call Mad Dog to tell him about the meeting instead of me, don't you think there's a chance that Jessie will find out about it?" I said.

"I guess so," said Fink.

"If she finds out I didn't do it, she'll know it's because I was too scared to do it myself," I told him.

"Oh, I see what you mean," Fink said.

"No point in adding fuel to the fire," I said.

"Let me guess, Nat-o, is that another one of your mom's expressions?" Fink asked.

"Yeah, sorry, you know how they just slip out sometimes. Anyway, you get what I'm saying, right?" I said.

"Yeah, but it's no big deal," Fink said. "I'll just imitate your voice when I make the call. He won't know the difference. He's never heard you talk on the phone. You've never called him before, have you?"

"Are you kidding?" I said.

As it turned out, Mad Dog wasn't home. His mom said he wouldn't be back until dinnertime.

"Could you please tell him there's a meeting of the Vasco da Gama group tomorrow at Jessie's house after school? Oh, and make sure to tell him it was Nat Boyd who called, okay?" Fink said, giving me a thumbs-up.

"That was brilliant!" I said, clapping him on the back after he hung up the phone. "If Jessie asks, he'll tell her I was the one who called, and you didn't even have to disguise your voice or anything."

"I told you not to worry. That's one problem down. Now let's talk about how we're going to handle Corn Bloomers," said Fink.

I liked the way Fink said "we." He wouldn't let me take on Jessie alone. We were a team.

"We have to think of a way to convince Corn Bloomers that you were only kidding when you told her you were scared of Mad Dog."

"How are we going to do that?" I asked. "I wasn't kidding, and you know it. If I even look at the guy, my teeth start chattering."

"For starters, maybe you better not look at him," said Fink.

"I usually don't. But we're going to be working in the same group. Don't you think Jessie will notice if I don't ever look at him?" I asked.

"I think she'll be more likely to notice if you

smell bad," Fink said. "Is it really true that he gives you B.O.?"

"I'm not sure, but I think it's possible," I said. "I definitely sweat when I'm scared and, as you know, he does scare me."

"Look, they make deodorant for a reason, don't they?" Fink said. "All you gotta do is wear some of that stuff whenever you're going to be around him and you should be okay."

"I don't know. I still think she's going to be able to tell," I said. "Even if I don't *smell* scared, what if I *look* scared? She's going to be watching me like a hawk. She'll notice."

"Not if I keep her distracted," said Fink.

"How are you going to do that?" I asked.

"I don't know. I'll think of something," he told me.

"Okay," I said.

Fink has a lot of good ideas, but I should have learned by now that I should always ask him exactly what he has in mind before I say okay to it.

That night I took my shower, and then I lay in bed

reading a biography of Vasco da Gama until my eyes got heavy and I drifted off. That's when it happened. Something that happens all the time, but that I've never told anybody about — not even Fink. *I had one of my dreams.* I heard somewhere that we all have a ton of dreams every single night, whether we remember them in the morning or not, but I have a feeling most people don't have the kind of dreams I do. Mine are always really weird and sometimes really embarrassing, too.

The dream I had that night was both — weird *and* embarrassing. I'm not going to tell you what it was about. After all, like I said, I don't even tell Fink about my dreams, and he's my best friend, but I will tell you this much: Jessie Kornblume was in it and she was wearing a big poofy white wedding dress. And don't bother to try to twist my arm, that's all I'm willing to tell.

At the meeting the next day at Jessie's house, the "something" Fink came up with to distract her was doing animal imitations. It might not have been such a bad idea, except that Fink can't *do* animal imitations. He tried to imitate a cow, a pig, a cat, a horse, and a chicken, but he was so bad at it, they all sounded exactly the same.

I have to admit, he did succeed in distracting Jessie. I mean, it was pretty hard to look at anything else in the room with Fink flapping and snorting all over the place. The problem was, Fink got so carried away doing his imitations that Mad Dog, who was sitting next to him on the couch, decided to move to another seat to get farther away from him. I've already told you that bad luck seems to follow me wherever I go, so I probably don't need to tell you where he decided to sit instead. Right next to me! Fink didn't even notice.

"And now here's my imitation of a woolly mammoth," he announced.

Before he could do it, though, Jessie reached over and clapped her hand over his mouth.

"Stop!" she yelled. "First of all, there's no way you could possibly know what a woolly mammoth sounds like because they've been extinct for two million years, and second, even if you did know, you couldn't imitate it because you can't even imitate a cat."

"I can so. I did my cat already, don't you remember?" Fink said.

"Yeah, I remember. It sounded exactly like your cow and your pig and all the rest of them," she said.

"If you think you're so great, let's hear *you* do a cat," said Fink.

"I could if I wanted to," said Jessie as she pushed her glasses up on her nose. "But I don't want to sink to your level. You're so low, you're subterranean."

Fink and Jessie glared at each other, and Mad Dog just sat there beside me like a great big lump. A great big way-too-close-for-comfort lump, to be exact. I wondered how long this meeting was going to last.

"Uh, you guys, since it doesn't look like we're going to get anything done here today, do you think maybe we should call this meeting off?" I asked.

"Fine with me," said Fink.

"Well, it's not fine with me," said Jessie. "I've made a list of study topics and assigned a different topic to each person in the group."

"Who put you in charge?" asked Fink.

"Somebody has to be in charge. Did *you* make a list of study topics?" Jessie asked.

"No, because I'm not a nerd with nothing better to do with my time than annoy people by acting like a big smarty-pants who thinks they're in charge of the world," said Fink.

"Oh, so instead, maybe I should spend my time doing crummy animal imitations that don't sound anything like the animals they're supposed to be. Would that be better?" said Jessie.

"If you ask me, it would," said Fink.

"Who asked you?" she said.

"Actually, you did," he said. Then he licked his finger and drew an imaginary line in the air because he knew he'd just scored a point.

I looked over at Mad Dog, just for a second, to see what he was making of all this. Big mistake. To my horror, he wasn't watching Fink and Jessie at all. He was staring straight at me, and the look on his face sent a prickle of electric fear shooting right up the back of my neck.

CHAPTER FOUR

I'm not a mind reader, but if someone had asked me to guess what Mad Dog was thinking as he sat there staring at me, I don't think I would have had much trouble. I was pretty sure he was thinking about squashing me like a bug. I wasn't sure *why* he wanted to squash me, especially since I'd pretty much never even talked to the guy. But he looked mad, and I decided I didn't really want to stick around to find out what his problem was with me. I got up and started walking toward the door.

"Hey, where do you think you're going?" asked Jessie.

"Nowhere. I'm just stretching my legs," I said. I

didn't want to tip off Mad Dog, in case he was planning to make a grab for me before I could escape, but I also didn't want Jessie to know I was scared. I felt something wet and warm slide down my ribs. Oh, great, I was starting to sweat.

"Sit down," Jessie said. "We have to go over the study topics."

The last thing I wanted to do was to sit down next to Mad Dog again. I was already sweating, and being that close to him was bound to make it worse. But I knew if I didn't sit back down, Jessie was going to know for sure what was going on. So I sat down as far over on the side of the chair as I could get without falling off.

The phone rang, and Jessie picked it up.

"Hello? Oh, hi, Marla," she said.

Fink crossed his eyes and made a face. I was careful not to because I was afraid Mad Dog might think I was making a face at him, and I didn't think I needed to give him another reason to hate my guts right then.

"I haven't decided yet, maybe the pink one with

the ruffles," Jessie said. "Or the turquoise with the fringe. What do you think?"

Fink rolled his eyes.

"No, you decide. It's your turn. Ruffles or fringe?" she said.

There are about a million things I don't get about girls. For instance, why do they play those games on the playground where they chant stuff and slap each other's hands? You know the ones I'm talking about? *"Down, down, baby, down by the roller coaster,"* and that other one about some girl named Mary who has a bunch of buttons down her back. I've seen them waste a whole recess period doing that junk. Why don't they play ball instead?

And here's another thing: Why do girls giggle? If Fink and I think something is funny, we just laugh, like *normal* people. Why can't girls do that instead of getting silly and flopping around like hysterical fish? The Red Devils do all of that stuff, giggling and hand-slapping, but one of the most annoying girly habits they have is that they like to come to school dressed in matching outfits.

Obviously, that day in Jessie's living room we were witnessing what goes into making it happen. I can't imagine calling Fink up on the phone to plan what we were going to wear the next day. "I don't know, Fink. Which do you think, T-shirts with holes under the arms, or T-shirts with grease stains on the front?" It would never happen in a million years.

"I'm warning you. If you keep talking about fringe and ruffles, I'm going to urp on your couch here," said Fink. "Tell your little twin that you're busy right now, will you? We want to get out of here already."

I couldn't have agreed with him more.

"I can't talk right now, Marla," Jessie said. "The natives are getting restless."

Marla must have said something "funny" after that, because Jessie giggled (of course) and then hung up.

"Hurry up and show us your dumb topics already," Fink said. "But I can tell you right now, if I don't like mine, I'm not doing it."

Jessie flipped open her notebook, which I noticed was very neat and had little dividers in between each section. She turned to a section marked with a pink divider, and I noticed the ink she'd used to make her list was a matching shade of pink. Yet another annoying girly thing. How do they come up with this stuff?

" 'Study Topics for Vasco da Gama by Jessie Louise Kornblume,' " she read out loud in her most smarty-pants voice.

Fink groaned. Jessie ignored him and went on.

"Jessie Kornblume's topic," she said.

"Don't you mean Jessie *Louise* Kornblume's topic?" interrupted Fink.

Jessie ignored him again and went on.

"My topic will be the voyages of Vasco da Gama, including destinations, routes taken, and lands discovered."

That was okay with me. It sounded like she'd picked a hard topic for herself, and also one where she could maybe draw a map or something, which would make the rest of us look good.

"Nathaniel Boyd's topic," Jessie continued, "is Vasco da Gama's personal history. When and where he was born, schools he attended, family history, when he died and how."

I was okay with that, too. I figured it would be fairly easy to find out all that kind of stuff either in an encyclopedia, on the Internet, or in one of the reference books on explorers that Mrs. West had on the big bookshelf in our classroom. Also, it didn't sound like any drawing would be required, which was good, since all I can draw are stick figures, and even those pretty much stink.

"Boyd Fink's topic: problems," Jessie said.

We all waited for her to say more, but that was it.

"What do you mean, problems?" Fink finally asked.

"Just what I said. Problems. I figured you'd be good at that, since you cause so many yourself," Jessie said.

"Me? I'm not the one who came up with these boring old topics," said Fink.

"Hey," I said, jumping in to keep it from heating up again and making this awful meeting take even longer. "Why don't you just explain what you mean by problems, Jessie, because I don't understand it, either."

"Why am I not surprised?" Jessie said as she pushed her glasses up again. I saw Fink imitate her out of the corner of my eye. He may be lousy at animal imitations, but he has Jessie down pretty well.

"Vasco da Gama encountered a lot of problems during his explorations," she said.

"He did? Like what, for instance?" Fink asked. "Whether to wear ruffles or fringe on his big voyage?"

"Very funny. Trust me, he encountered problems, and that's all I'm saying about it. Otherwise, I'll be doing all the work instead of you. Just look it up and write them down. Do you think you can handle that, or do I need to hold your hand?" she said.

"I'd rather die," Fink said.

"Personally, I'd rather eat worms," I said under my breath. Fink heard me and laughed out loud. I was about to laugh, too, but what happened next was the opposite of funny.

Mad Dog spoke for the first time since he'd gotten there, and what he said sent another hot prickle up my neck, even bigger than the one before.

"I want weapons," he said.

Weapons? I was a mind reader after all! Mad Dog

was planning to do me in. All he needed was the right weapon. I flashed back to that little mouse he'd stuffed in the gym shoe back in kindergarten and wondered what he had in mind for me. I guess Jessie and Fink must have been wondering the same thing because they were both sitting there looking kind of stunned. I couldn't move. I couldn't think straight. I was so freaked out, I couldn't even itch.

I don't know why, but all of a sudden for some reason my eyes fell on a framed photograph on the mantel that I hadn't noticed before. It was a wedding picture, and even from a distance it was pretty obvious that it was Jessie's parents. They looked different — Mr. Kornblume had hair, and Mrs. Kornblume was a lot thinner — but you could still tell it was them.

Mr. Kornblume was wearing a tuxedo and a big white bow tie, but it was what Mrs. Kornblume was wearing that made me gasp. I swear, it was the exact same poofy wedding gown Jessie had been wearing the night before in my dream. Seeing that dress made the whole embarrassing dream come rushing back to me, especially the parts I didn't tell you about before and am still not going to tell you about, no matter what. I felt my face turn red and another trickle of sweat roll down my ribs. I knew if I didn't get out of that room fast, I was going to be in very big trouble.

Too late.

"Hey, what's that funky smell?" asked Mad Dog, suddenly sniffing at the air. He lifted one of his giant arms over his head, sniffed himself, and announced, "It's not me."

Jessie and Fink both turned to look at me at the exact same moment.

"Ewww," said Jessie. "It's you, isn't it, Nat?"

"Did you forget to buy that deodorant we talked about?" Fink asked.

I couldn't believe he said that right out loud in front of everybody!

"Gross! Nat, you reek," Jessie wailed.

If I did, it wasn't because I'd forgotten about the deodorant. I was wearing three, count 'em, three layers of Manly Mint, which I'd bought at the drugstore with my allowance and then smeared under my arms right before I came over. I couldn't help it if Manly

Mint wasn't doing the job. My life was in danger. It's only natural to sweat when you think you're about to be stuffed into a gym shoe.

"I can't breathe," Jessie said as she waved her hand in front of her nose. "Somebody open a window."

"I'll do it," said Fink.

"No, wait, let me do it," I said quickly. Even though I was freaking out, I was clearheaded enough to know I needed a plan.

I tried to look, as my mother would say, "cool as a cucumber" as I walked toward the window. I put my hands in my pockets and whistled like I wasn't up to anything at all. I was really relieved that Mad Dog seemed to be buying my act. He didn't try to grab me or anything as I walked past him. Then, still whistling, I opened the window as wide as I could and without looking back, I pushed the curtains out of the way, jumped out the window, and ran for home as fast as I could.

CHAPTER FIVE

As I was running home, my mind was racing, too. Why was Mad Dog so mad at me? What had I done to tick him off? About halfway home, I started getting tired. I looked over my shoulder to see if anyone was chasing me, but nobody was there. I still wanted to get home, so to make myself run harder, I imagined that not only Mad Dog was chasing me, but so was Jessie, and she was wearing that poofy wedding dress. That worked. I don't think I've ever run faster in my life.

By the time I reached my house, I had a terrible cramp in my side and I was completely out of breath. As I stumbled up the front steps, I could see my mother through the window of her office, bending over a patient.

"You're doing a super job with your rubber bands!" I heard her say through the open window. "Three more weeks and we might be able to move you into a retainer."

My mother is Dr. Holly Boyd, the most popular orthodontist in Jeffersonville. She's either straightened, is in the process of straightening, or will someday probably straighten pretty much everybody's teeth in town. Her office is attached to our house. It has a separate entrance off the front porch and a big painted sign with a giant smile on it that says BOYD ORTHODONTICS. There is one other orthodontist in town, Dr. Pane, but nobody I know ever goes to him. Who can blame them? Would you want somebody with that name messing around with wires and pliers in *your* mouth?

My mom looked up and waved when she saw me standing there. I didn't want her to see how hard I was panting because I knew if she did, she might get worried and come out and start asking me a lot of questions. So I waved back and quickly went inside. I stood in the hallway for a minute, catching my breath, then I headed for the kitchen. When I'm nervous, I like to eat. I grabbed a bag of carrots out of the refrigerator and started crunching like there was no tomorrow (another one of my mother's cornball expressions, in case you couldn't tell). Of course, I would have preferred some cookies or chips to snack on, but Dr. Holly Boyd believes in healthy snacks, not just for her patients but for her family as well.

My mom and I are the whole family. Just us two. My dad isn't around anymore. He left when I was just a baby, and I don't have any brothers or sisters. I've got some cousins who live in Kansas City, and an Aunt Mozelle in Dallas, but other than that, it's just Mom and me. Oh, and my goldfish, Hercules. He only cost twenty-five cents because he had something called fin rot when I got him, which is why he was on sale. His fins are fine now, and even though the fish book says most goldfish only live for a few months, I've had Herc for two-and-a-half years already, and he's still going strong.

I had only been sitting there munching carrots for a few minutes when Fink called.

"Are you nuts?" he said. "Why did you jump out the window like that?"

"Why do you think I jumped out the window? Mad Dog was about to kill me, in case you didn't notice," I said.

"What are you talking about?" he said.

"Didn't you hear him? He said he wanted weapons," I said.

"Uh, Nat-man, I think we need to talk. Is it okay if I come over?" Fink asked, and from the sound of his voice I could tell it was something serious. Maybe he knew what Mad Dog had planned for me.

I timed Fink on the kitchen clock. It took him fifty-seven seconds to get here.

"What took you so long?" I asked him when he walked in the door.

"I had to put on my shoes. Quit complaining, I was tripping over myself all the way here because I didn't take any time to tie my laces," he said, holding up one foot with the long, white laces dangling.

"Never mind that now. What do you have to talk to me about? Is it about the weapons?" I asked nervously.

"Yeah, it's about the weapons," said Fink.

My heart was pounding and I was having trouble swallowing.

"Did he choose one?" I whispered hoarsely.

"Yeah, as his *topic*," said Fink.

"What do you mean, his topic?" I asked.

"He wants weapons to be his study topic," Fink said.

"*What?*" I said.

"He says he wants to study what weapons Vasco da Gama brought with him on his explorations," Fink explained.

"Are you kidding me?" I said.

"Nope," he said. "You jumped out the window and ran away from a study topic."

I knew what Fink was trying to say. That I had made a total fool of myself, running away from some innocent little study topic, but I didn't care. I was so relieved the weapons weren't intended for me.

"I must have been imagining the whole thing. Isn't that great? He doesn't hate me. I bet he wasn't even really looking at me funny the way I thought he was. He was probably just sitting there daydreaming about Vasco da Gama's weapons. This is so great. Here, have a carrot to celebrate," I said, pushing the bag of carrots toward Fink.

"I'd rather have a cookie," he said as he shoved the carrots back in my direction. "Got any?"

"In your dreams," I said. "But my mom probably has some of those health food bars in the cupboard. Want one?"

"No, thanks," he said. "I'm not in the mood for sawdust and dirt sprinkles."

"I feel so good right now I probably wouldn't even mind eating one of those things." I laughed.

"Hey, Nat-man, I don't want to bum you out or anything, but before you get too overjoyed, I think there's something you might want to think about," he said.

"What?" I asked, and right on cue my knee started to itch.

"Well, a certain redheaded person, whose name I don't even want to say because she makes me so sick, was there just now when you jumped out the window," he said. "That probably wasn't the smartest thing to do right in front of her, don't you think?"

I'd forgotten all about Jessie.

"Knowing her, she's probably already on the phone with Marla blabbing about the whole thing. She's going to know for sure how I feel about Mad Dog now. I'm doomed all over again," I groaned.

"Not so fast," Fink said. "Let's think positive here. You know and I know that the reason you jumped out the window was because of Mad Dog. But Jessie doesn't know that."

"She doesn't?" I asked.

"Well, not for sure. All we have to do is come up with a good excuse for why you did it, to throw her off track," said Fink.

"Okay. Got any ideas?" I asked.

"Sure. You could tell her it was an accident. You meant to go out the door, but you got mixed up and went out the window instead," he suggested.

46

"Uh, no offense, but that's really dumb," I said.

"So's your thumb," he answered back as usual.

Once again, I was not in the mood for the rhyming game.

"Not now, Fink. Come on, what am I going to tell her?" I asked.

"Tell her that you suddenly remembered you had something important to do for your mom," he said.

"Isn't she going to ask me why I didn't just say that and then walk out the door like a normal person?" I asked.

"Tell her the window was closer," he said.

Actually, that wasn't too bad. I mean, at least it was sort of logical. I could have remembered something I needed to do, and the window really had been a lot closer to me than the door. She might buy that. Yeah, why shouldn't she believe that?

"Thanks, Fink," I said.

"No problem," he told me.

Later that night, when I went to bed, I had trouble falling asleep. On the one hand, I felt good about the fact that I'd been wrong about Mad Dog being after me; but on the other hand, I was worried about how Jessie was going to be the next day. I lay there thinking for a long time until finally I was sleepy enough to doze off. And that's when it happened. Another one of my dreams.

This time I was standing on the deck of a huge wooden sailing ship. The wind was howling and the ship was being tossed around like a piece of driftwood in the crashing waves. I was hanging onto a rope, trying to keep from getting washed overboard. Another guy was hanging onto a rope next to me, and when I looked at him more closely, I realized it was Vasco da Gama. I knew it was him because he looked just the way I'd seen him in a picture in one of Mrs. West's books. He had a long beard and a velvet hat with a big feather in it, and he looked worried.

"What's the matter, Vasco?" I asked.

"I've got problems," he said. "I'm trying to find a waterway to India."

"You think *you've* got problems?" I said. "Not only am I in danger of being washed overboard in the middle of this terrible storm, but on top of that, Jessie

Kornblume knows I'm afraid of Mad Dog and she's going to tell everyone at school."

Vasco stroked his little beard thoughtfully. "That is serious," he said. "Tell me something, this Jessie Kornblume of yours, does she wear glasses and walk around wearing a poofy wedding dress?"

"Yes, but please don't tell anybody," I said.

"Don't worry," he said. "I couldn't even if I wanted to. Remember, I died in 1524?"

"Listen, Vasco, can I ask you something?" I said. "Are you afraid of anything?"

Vasco da Gama looked around for a minute to make sure no one was listening, then he leaned in and whispered in my ear.

"Pirates make me sweat."

"Really?" I said. "You must have done a pretty good job of hiding that because I haven't seen that anywhere in any of the books I've read about you."

"Hold on!" he shouted as a huge wave crashed onto the deck, soaking us both with cold seawater.

"Do you have any advice for how to keep people from finding out something embarrassing like that about you?" I shouted to him over the roar of the powerful storm. "I could really use your help."

He didn't answer. And a minute later when the giant wave receded, I found myself alone on the deck. Vasco da Gama had vanished, washed away before he could answer my question.

CHAPTER SIX

"You look crummy," Fink said when we met up on the corner to walk to school the next morning.

"Gee, thanks," I said.

"No, really. You don't look like yourself. What's the matter, are you sick or something?" he asked.

"No, I just didn't sleep very well last night. Do you really think Jessie's going to buy that excuse we came up with yesterday?" I asked.

"Of course she will," said Fink.

"Are you sure?" I asked.

"Positive," he said.

When it comes to his ideas, Fink is very confident. Sometimes a little too confident. Plus, I guess I wanted to believe him, since Vasco da Gama and I hadn't come up with anything better to tell her.

Jessie and Marla were standing on the playground, playing clapping games when we got to school, and I could tell from the way they lit up when they saw me that they'd been waiting for me.

Jessie didn't lose any time getting right to the point.

"Hey, Nat," she called out, "why'd you jump out the window yesterday in the middle of our meeting?"

Fink nudged me with his elbow.

"Go ahead, Nat-o. Lay it on her," he whispered.

"I forgot I had something important to do for my mom, and the window was closer than the door," I called back.

"You don't expect me to believe that, do you?" Jessie said with a mean laugh.

"Yeah, you don't expect us to believe that, do you?" Marla said.

"What do you know about it, Marla?" Fink said. "You weren't even there."

"I know plenty. Jessie told me he stunk up her living room, and then he jumped out the window and ran away," said Marla.

"You heard what he said, he had something important he had to do," Fink said.

"Yeah, like hide under his bed and cry like a baby," Jessie teased.

"Was it stinky under there, Mr. Scaredy-cat?" asked Marla, with a giggle.

"The only things around here that Nat is scared of are your ugly faces," Fink said, jumping to my defense, but they weren't listening. They were too busy giggling and pointing at me while they plugged their noses and waved their hands around like they were smelling something bad. I could tell it was going to be a very long day.

The bell rang and we all went into school, but of course the teasing didn't stop when we got to class. Whenever I walked past, one or the other of the Red Devils would say "P.U." or call me a scaredy-cat. It was pretty bad, but as bad as it was, there was something even worse going on. Mad Dog was still acting really weird, and it definitely wasn't my imagination. He was glaring at me like he hated my guts. But why?

"I don't get it," I told Fink. "What did I do to deserve this all of a sudden? He didn't used to hate me. He used to just ignore me."

Fink looked over at Mad Dog.

"That is not a friendly look," he said. "You must have done something to tick him off."

"What? I can't think of anything," I said.

Fink looked over at Mad Dog again.

Then he squinted a little and tilted his head to one side, as though he was studying something. "You ever look at Mad Dog's teeth?" he asked.

"Not if I can help it, why?" I said.

"He's got dog teeth," Fink said. "Sort of, you know, sharp and snaggly and yellow. And when he smiles, it kind of looks like when a dog smiles."

"Dogs don't smile," I said.

"Sure they do. Don't you think dogs ever feel happy?" Fink said.

"Of course they feel happy. That's why they wag their tails," I answered.

"They smile, too," Fink said. "All animals do."

"All animals?" I asked.

Fink nodded.

"Even fish?" I said.

"Sure, fish can smile," Fink said.

"Now I know you don't know what you're talking about. Remember, I've got a fish, and I know for a fact Herc never smiles," I said.

"Maybe he's depressed," said Fink.

"He is not," I said. "He's happy. He's just a fish and fish don't smile."

"Sharks do," Fink said.

"They do not. They show their teeth when they bite stuff. Showing your teeth is not the same thing as smiling," I said. "How did we get into this, anyway?"

"Mad Dog's teeth," Fink said.

"Oh, yeah. Forget about whether or not fish smile, will you? You've got to help me figure out why Mad Dog hates me so much."

"Maybe you should just ask him," said Fink.

"Oh, another great idea from Mr. Fink. I think I'll walk over to him right now and say, 'Gee, Mad Dog, would you mind telling me why you hate my guts all of a sudden? And while you're at it, maybe you'd like to take a swing at me since I'm standing here right up close, making it easy for you to sink your fist into my face.'"

"It was just a suggestion. You don't have to bite my head off, Boyd," Fink said.

"I'm sorry. I'm just a little freaked out. I mean, seriously, have you looked at Mad Dog's arms lately? They're like huge caveman clubs. And his hands are the size of catcher's mitts."

"I wouldn't know about that," said Fink.

Fink doesn't play any sports. No baseball, no basketball, no soccer. Not even Ping-Pong. His parents think it's too dangerous, so instead, he plays the clarinet. Fink's mom and dad are what my mother calls "a smidge overprotective," which means basically they don't let him do anything fun. On Saturday mornings, when all the boys in Jeffersonville are out on the ball fields, Fink is at Mrs. Percy O. Danforth's house playing in a woodwind quintet.

"Are you any good?" I remember asking him once.

"No. I'm hopeless," he told me. "Even Mrs. Danforth says so."

"She says you're hopeless?" I asked.

"No. She says I lack *musical prowess*."

"What does that mean?" I asked.

"It means I'm hopeless," Fink said.

All morning I could feel Mad Dog staring at me, like his eyes were burning little red-hot holes in the back of my head. And then at lunch, instead of sitting in his usual seat in the corner, he sat at the table right across from where Fink and I always sit. He'd never done that before, and it made me so nervous I could barely choke down my lunch. Mad Dog didn't eat anything. He spent the whole lunch hour staring at me — first in the lunchroom and then out on the playground.

"What did I do?" I asked Fink when the lunch bell finally rang and we headed back inside to class.

"I don't know, maybe he just doesn't like the way you look or something," Fink said.

"He wasn't staring at me last week, " I said. "Do I look any different now than I did then?"

Fink looked at me and shook his head.

"Not really," he said. "Your hair's a little longer. Or maybe it's just flat because it's dirty."

"My hair isn't dirty," I said. "I washed it last night, and besides, even if it was dirty, is that a reason for Mad Dog to hate me? He's not exactly Mr. Personal Hygiene, in case you haven't noticed."

"True," said Fink. "Well, the only thing I can think of is that you must have insulted him and he found out about it somehow," Fink said.

"You're the only one I've ever talked to about him, and you never told him anything I said, did you?" I asked.

"Of course not," said Fink. "So it has to be something else. Something you did."

I racked my brain, but I couldn't come up with one single thing I could have done to make Mad Dog mad at me. The bell rang for the end of lunch hour.

"Man, I really don't feel like going back in there," I said as Fink and I walked up the steps of the school.

"I don't blame you," said Fink. "I wish I could think of a way to help you out. But unless we can figure out what he's mad about, it's going to be kind of hard to figure out how to make him un-mad."

I hadn't gotten anything done all morning. Between Jessie and Marla teasing me, and Mad Dog giving me the evil eye, I'd been too distracted to do any work. How could I concentrate on Vasco da Gama's life when I was worrying about my own? After lunch, things got better, though. For one thing, Mad Dog wasn't in class.

"Mr. Ditmeyer had an appointment, so he has been excused early today," Mrs. West explained to the class.

Boy, were those words music to my ears. I breathed a huge sigh of relief. With Mad Dog gone, all I had to deal with was Jessie and Marla. The worst of the day was over. At least, that's what I thought.

CHAPTER SEVEN

The rest of the school day actually did go pretty well. Mrs. West caught Marla and Jessie teasing me and called them up to her desk to have a "little chat." Little chats with Mrs. West usually mean she tells you to knock off doing whatever annoying thing you're doing or she'll make you stay after school and wash desks.

After the teasing stopped, and with Mad Dog gone, I felt relaxed enough to actually get some work done. I read an interesting chapter about Vasco da Gama in one of the reference books and took some notes. I found out da Gama was born in Portugal in the mid-1400s. I guess people didn't make a big deal about birthdays at that time, because nobody remembers the actual date he was born. I'm glad I didn't live back then; I'd hate it if people forgot my birthday. It's the one day of the year my mother puts no limits on sugar, and I always eat about a million cupcakes with tons of chocolate frosting on them.

My stomach rumbled. I guess thinking about those cupcakes reminded me that I hadn't eaten much lunch. I'd been too upset about Mad Dog staring at me in the lunchroom. It sure was a lot nicer now that he was gone. I wished he could have appointments every day.

Fink was on the computer looking up stuff about da Gama's problems, and Jessie was busy working on a map. I got up to go sharpen my pencil.

"Hey, Fink," I said as I walked past him on my way up to the front of the room. "Vasco da Gama was afraid of pirates, did you know that? Maybe that was one of his problems."

"Where'd you read that?" he asked.

"Uh, nowhere exactly," I said. I didn't want to tell Fink that Vasco had told me that himself, the night before in my dream. "I just heard it somewhere."

Fink gave me a funny look, but he didn't say anything. I sharpened my pencil, and on the way back to my desk I stopped to look at Jessie's map. Even though she'd been making me miserable all day, I have to admit the map looked really great. Instead of using white paper, like I probably would have, she was drawing on yellowish paper that she'd torn all the edges off of so that it looked like it was really old and beat up.

With stuff like that map and the research Fink and I were busy doing, I was beginning to think we had a pretty good chance of getting an A from Mrs. West on our project. I thought it would be nice if at least one good thing came out of this awful experience. I was thinking about that A as I leaned over Jessie's desk.

"Your map looks pretty cool," I told her.

She looked up and smiled, and for a minute I thought maybe she was going to say something normal and nice like "Thanks." Instead, she pointed behind me and whispered, "Don't look now, Nat, but here comes Mad Dog, and I think he's after you!"

Of course I turned around to look. Wouldn't you? But Mad Dog was nowhere in sight. It was a trick. I'd fallen for it — hook, line, and sinker — as my mother would say.

My mother also says that someday when I'm older I'll probably meet a wonderful woman and fall in love with her and decide to get married and all of that other mushy, Valentiney stuff, but she's dead wrong about that. No matter how nice any woman ever is, I'll never be able to like her because I'll know that she was once a girl, and as far as I'm concerned there's nothing worse in the whole world than girls — and that includes rattlesnakes and smelly cheese.

Marla and Jessie tried to sneak in a couple more attacks on me that afternoon. But after a while I could tell by the look in their eyes when it was about to happen, and I'd get out of the way, fast. When I wasn't watching, Fink kept an eye out for me and warned me whenever he saw either one of them coming too close.

"Red alert! Danger approaching on your left," he'd whisper. Or, "Double trouble from the rear!" I felt like one of those divers in a shark cage with great whites coming at me from every side, only these man-eaters had freckles and red hair. It was exhausting.

After school, Jessie came over to where Fink and I were standing.

"What now?" I sighed.

"Don't worry, I'll handle this, Nat-o," Fink said. "What do you want, Corn Bloomers?"

"I want to have another meeting of our explorer group," she told us.

"Another meeting? Why?" said Fink. "We all know what we're supposed to be doing. You saw us both working today. Who needs another meeting?"

"I sure don't," I said.

"I think we should get together so we can check on everyone's progress," she said.

"Why do you always have to use words like *progress*?" Fink asked. "Didn't anybody ever tell you that's a *teacher* word, not a *kid* word? Why don't you try talking like what you are for a change?"

"Why don't you try talking like what you are, too, and make monkey noises?" Jessie said. "Oops, I forgot. You can't do animal imitations, can you? Never mind."

I knew she was going to push up her glasses after that zinger.

"By the way, if you don't agree to having another meeting, I'm going to tell Mrs. West that you two are not cooperating," she sniffed.

"You have no right," Fink said.

"You have no choice," Jessie said.

"Oh, yeah? Well, you have no *musical prowess*."

"What's that supposed to mean?" she asked, and I could tell from the little quiver in her voice that Fink had actually gotten to her.

I had to laugh. I knew exactly what was bothering Jessie. She was embarrassed. She might have scored a 99.9 on the Farnsworth, but Miss Know-it-all didn't know what *musical prowess* meant. Fink might be hopeless on clarinet, but he'd just gotten Jessie right where it hurts.

"Guess you'd better run home and look that up in your dictionary, huh?" I said.

Jessie had been teasing me all day and making her take a turn on the other end of it was too hard to resist. I should have known it wouldn't stay like that for very long, though.

"I've been meaning to ask you, Nat, do you know what *defenestration* means?" she asked.

"De-fena — what?" I said.

"De-fen-es-tra-tion," she repeated slowly. "You really ought to know what it means since you've got a bad case of it, and I hear it can be fatal."

She pushed up her glasses and started to walk away. Then she stopped and turned back to us.

"I'm calling a meeting for tomorrow afternoon," she said. "Four o'clock at Nat's house."

"My house? Why should it be at my house?" I objected.

"Because we had the first meeting at my house and now it's somebody else's turn," Jessie said. "Besides, if it's at your house, you can't jump out the window and run home because you'll already be home."

"But —" I started to say.

"But nothing," interrupted Jessie. "Four o'clock tomorrow afternoon at your house. Be there, or else."

CHAPTER EIGHT

Even though the line was really long, Fink insisted that we stop at the Bee Hive snack bar so he could get a milk shake on the way home from school. My mom doesn't let me have those, so I got a cup of ice water.

"Are we going to let old Corn Bloomers order us around like that?" Fink asked as he tore off one end of his paper straw wrapper and shot the other end at me. He missed me by a mile.

"I don't know," I said, doing the same with my straw and hitting him right in the middle of his forehead. "What can we do? If we don't let her call the dumb meeting, she's definitely going to tattle to Mrs. West."

"Oh, let her tattle," said Fink. "Mrs. West knows Jessie's a great big tattletale. She won't listen to her. She'll make Jessie have another 'little chat' with her."

"We don't know that for sure. What if Mrs. West believes her, and we end up being the ones who have to have the 'little chat,'" I said.

"For what? What did we do?" Fink asked.

"We haven't done anything. Not yet, anyway. But if Jessie tells her she wanted to have a meeting and we refused, well, that's something, isn't it?" I said.

"Which is worse — getting in trouble with Mrs. West or having to have another meeting with Jessie and Mad Dog?" asked Fink.

This was not an easy question to answer.

"Let's look at the pros and cons of it," I said.

"The what of it?" he asked.

"The pros and cons," I said. "You know, the good versus the bad."

"Is this another one of those sports things? You

keep forgetting I don't get that stuff, Boyd. As you just saw, I can't even aim a straw wrapper," Fink said.

"Relax, Fink, it's not about sports. All I'm saying is, it will be bad if we don't show up for the meeting, because Jessie will get mad and go to Mrs. West, and we might get in trouble. And it will also be bad if we do show up for the meeting, because what if the B.O. thing happens again? I mean, you saw how Mad Dog was looking at me today. Anything could happen."

"All we've got so far is cons," Fink said. "Aren't there any pros?"

"Let me think. Okay, here's one. Even though it will be boring and Mad Dog will probably be giving me dirty looks the whole time, if we have the meeting, maybe we can make some progress with our presentation and get a good grade on it," I said.

"Do I have an ear wax problem, or did you just say *progress*?" Fink asked. "You're scaring me, Nat-man. That sounds like something Corn Bloomers would say. The next thing you know, you'll be telling me to *cooperate* or you'll *lodge a complaint*."

"Or worse. I'll be calling you up to see what you want to wear to school tomorrow so we can match," I said.

We were both laughing as we turned the corner and headed down our street.

"I've been thinking about something," Fink said. "I feel really bad about what happened this morning. I really did think Jessie would buy that excuse about the window being closer. So to make up for it, I came up with an idea for something you can do to absolutely guarantee that Jessie will quit teasing you about being afraid of Mad Dog."

"Please don't tell me it's something crazy like an armpit transplant," I said.

"Nope. It's a sleepover," Fink said.

"A sleepover?" I said.

"Yeah. At your house. With Mad Dog," said Fink.

"Are you insane?" I shouted. "I'm not having Mad Dog come for a sleepover. Do you think I'd feel safe sleeping in the same room as that guy? He hates my guts."

"You have to admit, if Jessie knew you had him sleep over, there's no way she'd think you were scared of him," Fink said.

"Yeah, but I think you're forgetting something," I said. "I *am* scared of him."

We were in front of Fink's house by then, so he asked me if I wanted to come in and hang out for a while.

"No, thanks," I said. "I want to get home. I'm waiting for something to come in the mail. If it's here, maybe today won't be a total loss after all."

"What's coming in the mail?" asked Fink.

"Tadpoles," I told him.

"Real ones?" asked Fink.

"Yeah, my mom said I could send away for them, and it's supposed to take six to eight weeks. It'll be six weeks today."

"What are you going to do with tadpoles?" Fink asked.

"Watch them turn into frogs," I said.

"Cool. Then what?" he asked.

"Let them go, I guess," I answered.

"Also cool. Call me if you get them and I'll come over to see them," Fink said.

"Why? So you can tell me they're depressed, like my fish?" I said.

"Very funny. Call me," he said, and he headed up his front walk. Before he went in, he turned and called back to me, "Think about that sleepover thing, will you? I'm telling you, it would work. Later, Nat Boyd."

"Later, Boyd Fink," I called back.

I started walking toward my house, but as I got closer, I saw something that made me stop dead in my tracks. Somebody was sitting on my front steps. Somebody I recognized right away even from a distance. It was Mad Dog! But what was he doing on my steps? Was he waiting for me? Was he planning to pound me right in front of my own house? I quickly hid behind a bush, where I could watch him, but he couldn't see me.

He had something in his hands. A small white box with writing on it. All of a sudden I realized what it was. My tadpoles! I'd waited six long weeks for them, and now there they were in Mad Dog's evil clutches. As I watched in horror, Mad Dog stood up, shook his head, and then jammed the box of tadpoles roughly under his arm. As he walked away, he spit on my steps.

I waited until he was out of sight, then I came out from behind the bush, ran home, and called Fink.

"That creep just kidnapped my tadpoles!" I told him.

"I'll be right there," he said.

Fifty-nine seconds later he walked in.

"Sorry it took me so long. I had to finish the sandwich my mom made me before she'd let me leave," he explained. "Now, tell me everything. How do you know Mad Dog stole your tadpoles?" Fink asked me.

"I saw him with my own two eyes," I said. "He took the box right off my porch."

"Are you sure it was him?" he asked.

"Do you know anybody else with caveman club arms and hands like catcher's mitts?" I asked.

Fink shook his head.

"And you know what he did before he ran off with the box? He spit on my porch," I said.

"Gross. Show me," Fink said.

We went out on the steps to look at Mad Dog's spit, but we couldn't find it.

"Maybe it evaporated," I said.

"If we call the FBI, they can come over and run some DNA tests on the cement to trace it to him," Fink suggested. "They always do that on TV."

"I don't think the FBI is going to care enough about my tadpoles to come test Mad Dog's spit, do you?" I said.

"Probably not, but they should," Fink said. "After all, those tadpoles were a bunch of innocent stolen babies. Frog babies, but babies just the same."

"What do you think he's going to do with them?" I asked.

"Knowing him, he'll probably eat them," Fink said.

"Or put them in somebody's gym shoe," I added sadly.

"Don't you think your mom would buy you more

tadpoles if you told her what happened to this batch?" Fink asked.

"I don't know," I said. "They were pretty expensive, and I had to beg her for a long time before she agreed to let me get them."

"Maybe you should tell her what's been going on, you know, about Mad Dog being weird with you and everything," Fink said.

"I'm not sure that's a good idea," I said.

"Why not? I'm sure she'd take your side," said Fink.

"Yeah, but remember when that creepy little girl with the big forehead, Leslie Zebac, had a crush on you in kindergarten and chased you all around the playground trying to hug you?" I asked.

"Yeah, what about it?" Fink said.

"Remember how you told your mom, and then she called up Leslie's mom, and they made you guys have a powwow to discuss your feelings?" I said.

"I forgot that's what they called it, but you're right, they made us have a powwow. How dorked out is *that*? But why are you bringing this all up now?" asked Fink.

"I'm trying to make a point. Did getting your mother involved make it better or worse?" I asked.

"Much worse," he said. "That powwow idea totally backfired. Leslie Zebac told everybody in our class that I'd invited her over to play at my house, and after that they all thought I liked her. Some of them probably still think it."

"See, that's what I mean, it's not always safe to let your mom get involved in your business," I said.

"I hear ya," said Fink. He walked into the kitchen, grabbed a clean glass out of the cupboard, and went to the refrigerator to get some juice. On the door was a note from my mother. He pulled it off and read it to me:

Ortho emerge. Nuke the mac, eat something green, and do hw. I'll be home by 7.
Love, Mom

"What's an ortho emerge?" Fink asked.

"Orthodontic emergency," I explained. "Usually it's boring junk like a broken bracket or a popped wire. But one time I remember this goofy kid got his braces stuck to the TV antenna, and my mom had to go all the way out to his house to cut him loose," I said.

"Up on the roof?" Fink asked.

"No, it was one of those antennas that hooks onto the back of the TV and sits on top of it," I told him.

"What was the kid doing with the antenna in his mouth?" Fink asked.

"He discovered that when he smiled near the TV with his braces on, the reception got better. His sister wanted to watch some show on a cable channel, only they didn't have cable, so she talked him into putting his teeth right on the antenna to try to make the reception better, and the braces got stuck in the wires."

"Awesome," said Fink.

"Yeah, but like I told you, it's usually just a broken bracket," I said. "You wanna stay for dinner?"

"That depends. What's for dinner?"

"You read the note. I'm nuking some macaroni and cheese in the microwave," I said. "Plus, I have to have something green."

"We could put green food coloring on marshmallows. My mom sometimes does that on Saint Patrick's Day. It turns your teeth and lips bright green when you eat them. Pretty cool."

"I think my mother meant peas or lettuce, not green marshmallows. Besides, do you think she'd have marshmallows around? She doesn't even have cookies."

"Oh, yeah, I forgot," he said.

"It's okay, though. I know how much you hate vegetables, but I don't mind them. The note only says *I* have to eat something green, not you, so you're off the hook."

"That's good," he said.

Fink looked at the note again.

"I guess hw is homework, right?" he asked.

"Yeah," I said.

"We could do that math sheet together. I'll call and ask my mom if I can stay," he said. "And I hope she says yes, because I think we're having leftover meatloaf at my house, and I didn't even like it the first time around."

Fink stayed for dinner. We did our homework,

then we heated up the macaroni and cheese, and took it out on the back porch to eat it. Fink downed his dinner in about three bites, but I wasn't hungry.

"What's the matter?" Fink asked.

"I can't stop thinking about my tadpoles," I said. "I keep wondering if they're okay. You don't really think he'd eat them, do you?"

"Well," said Fink, "let me put it this way. There aren't too many people I think would be capable of eating tadpoles, but if I had to come up with one, it would probably be Mad Dog."

Unfortunately, I had to agree.

CHAPTER NINE

"There's no point in sitting around here worrying about those tadpoles, Nat. The thing to do is to get them back," he said.

"How?" I asked. "I can't just go over to his house and ask him to give them back. He'll pound me."

"You could invite him for a sleepover and tell him to bring any tadpoles he happens to have lying around. That would solve two of your problems at the same time," Fink said. My mother would have called that "killing two birds with one stone," but I managed not to say it.

"I'm *not* having Mad Dog for a sleepover, got that?" I said. "So quit bringing it up."

"Suit yourself," said Fink. "Where's your class list?"

"Right here," I said, pulling the list of the names and addresses of all the kids in our class off the bulletin board and handing it to Fink.

"Now give me the phone," Fink said.

"Who are you going to call?" I asked as I handed Fink the phone.

"Mad Dog," he said.

"*What?*" I tried to grab the phone away from him, but he was already dialing the number. "Why are you calling him? If you accuse him of taking the tadpoles, he's just going to deny it. I saw him, but I don't have any proof."

"Look. Do you want the tadpoles back or not?" Fink asked.

"Of course I do. But I don't want to take a chance on making Mad Dog even madder at me than he already is," I said.

"Calm down. I'm not going to do something as obvious as come right out and accuse him of stealing them. Give me a little credit here, I'm much more clever than that," said Fink. "I'm going to make him *want* to give them back."

"How? By hypnotizing him?" I asked.

"No, something way better. I'm going to guilt-trip him," said Fink.

"What's a guilt trip?" I asked.

"Okay, here's how it works: There are a lot of different kinds, but the basic guilt trip is when you make someone feel so bad about not doing what you want them to do that the only way they can feel okay again is to do exactly what you wanted them to do in the first place."

"That sounds pretty complicated," I said. "Are you sure you know how to do it?"

"I learned from a master. If guilt-tripping was an Olympic sport, trust me, my mother could win a gold medal without any problem," Fink said.

"She guilt-trips you?" I said.

"At least once a day," said Fink.

"I'm not sure I get what it is yet. Give me an example," I said.

"Okay. Here's one from last night: *Honey, I under-*

stand completely if you don't want to eat your meat loaf. I would never force a child of mine to eat something he doesn't care for. But before I take your plate away and dump your dinner down the disposal, I just think you should know I went all the way to the other side of town to Ralph's Market to get the best meat, and then I slaved over a hot stove all afternoon making that meat loaf for you. Not that you should care, but I actually burned my finger taking it out of the oven, too. See? See the little blister?" he said, imitating his mother's high-pitched voice and holding out his pinkie finger to me.

"So let me guess. Even though you hate meat loaf, you ate it anyway, because you felt guilty that she burned her finger making it for you?" I said.

"Bingo," said Fink. "A classic guilt trip."

"That's impressive," I said. "But do you really think you could guilt-trip Mad Dog into giving back my tadpoles?"

"Watch me work. I'll have him eating out of my hand before you know it," Fink said.

I have to say I actually felt hopeful as I watched

him finish dialing the phone number and wait while it rang. He really seemed like he knew what he was doing.

"Hello, Mad Dog?" he said into the phone. "This is Boyd Fink. Yeah, so, listen, the reason I'm calling is because I need your help. It's about Nathaniel Boyd. You know, Nat? Well, there's something wrong with him. Really wrong."

I didn't get it. How was telling Mad Dog there was something wrong with me going to make him want to give me back my tadpoles?

"See, he has this fatal disease," Fink went on.

How weird. That made the second time in two days someone had said I had a fatal disease. Jessie had told me I had de-fena-something-or-other and now Fink was telling Mad Dog I was sick, too. I was about to ask what he was doing, but the minute I opened my mouth, Fink motioned for me to be quiet. As I listened, he told Mad Dog the most incredible story.

"It's this rare disease, so rare it doesn't even have

a name, but the good news is, they think they might have a cure for it," Fink told him.

He told Mad Dog that the cure for my disease was tadpoles. He told him that I needed to put live tadpoles all over my skin and lie there completely still while they wriggled around and that as far as they knew that was the only hope I had. And then came the guilt-tripping part.

"See, the tadpoles were supposed to arrive in the mail today. And Nat is feeling sicker than ever, so he really needs them right away. But they didn't come. The post office says they must have gotten lost in the mail or delivered to the wrong address or something, so I'm calling everybody I know to see whether or not they accidentally got mailed some tadpoles today," Fink said. "Did you?"

So there it was. Fink's solution to my problem. He told Mad Dog that I was probably going to die unless I got a bunch of live tadpoles to wriggle all over my body. He hoped that when he heard that, Mad Dog would feel so guilty about stealing my tadpoles that he'd tell Fink they'd been delivered to his house by mistake and then run right over with them so he could give them back in time to save my life.

Fink stood there with the phone in his hand and listened quietly for a minute after he'd finished telling his story. Then he hung up.

"So? Did it work?" I asked him anxiously.

"Not exactly," said Fink.

"Did he feel guilty?" I asked.

"Not exactly," said Fink.

"Did he at least admit that he had the tadpoles?" I asked.

"Not exactly," said Fink.

"Well, what did he say exactly?" I asked.

"You want me to tell you *exactly* what he said?" asked Fink.

"Yes," I said. "Exactly."

Fink was looking at my leg. I hadn't even noticed that I'd begun to scratch.

"Are you sure you want me to tell you?" he asked.

"Tell me already!" I shouted.

"Okay, okay. After I told him all that stuff about you being sick and needing the tadpoles and everything, he said, um, well, he said —"

"What?" I said, grabbing him by the sleeve, "He said what?"

"He said, 'Tell Nathaniel Boyd if he says one word, I'm gonna get him,'" Fink said solemnly.

CHAPTER TEN

"So much for your wonderful guilt-tripping, huh?" I said.

"I'm sorry, Nat-o. I've never seen it fail before," Fink said. "I guess I should have had my mom do it."

"This is unbelievable," I said, reaching down and scratching my knee, which had been itching nonstop since Fink had gotten off the phone. "This day just keeps getting worse and worse. Mad Dog hates me for some mysterious reason, Jessie knows I'm scared of him and is never going to stop teasing me about it, and my tadpoles have been kidnapped. What's next?"

"Instead of worrying about that, I think the best thing for you to do right now is try to get your mind off your problems," Fink said. "What you need is a little distraction."

"Don't even *think* about doing imitations for me," I said.

"How about a game of Monopoly?" he said. "I'll even let you be the shoe."

For some reason, Fink loves being the shoe whenever we play. I didn't feel like playing a game, though.

"How about we watch TV, then?" he asked as he grabbed the newspaper and turned to the TV section in the back. "That movie *Toy Terror* is on. It just started. It's one of my favorites! You know the one about the teddy bear that goes crazy and starts chasing all the little kids around the playground until that one kid pokes a hole in him and he comes unstuffed?" said Fink.

"I'm not exactly in the mood for a movie about kids getting chased around by angry beasts at the moment," I said.

"Oh. Sorry," Fink said, putting down the paper. "Hey, did I tell you I finally came up with a great nickname for Marla? You know how her last name is

Dundee? Well, how about Marla Undies — you know, Dundee, undies?"

I shrugged. I just wasn't in the mood to laugh.

"What do you think my tadpoles are doing right now?" I asked sadly.

"You have to stop thinking about them, Nat-man," he said. "It's just going to bum you out more."

"I can't help it. I wonder if he even knows what to feed them," I said.

"What do they eat?" he asked.

"They like lettuce," I said. "But not raw lettuce. You have to boil it for fifteen minutes and then chop it up and keep it in the freezer. Then you sprinkle a little bit in the tank at a time so the water doesn't get too mucky for them."

"How do you know all this?" Fink asked.

"I read all about tadpoles on the Internet after I ordered them. I've got a whole bag of frozen lettuce in the freezer right now. Want to see?" I asked.

Fink followed me over to the refrigerator, where I got the plastic bag full of frozen lettuce out of the freezer to show him.

"Yeah, that looks like frozen lettuce all right," he said. "Yuck. All I can say is, I sure am glad I'm not a tadpole."

I looked sadly at the bag of lettuce I'd so carefully prepared.

"I hope Mad Dog doesn't starve the poor little things to death," I said. "You don't suppose he knows about them liking lettuce, do you?"

"Look, since the guilt-tripping didn't exactly work out the way I planned, and you don't seem to be able to think about anything other than those tadpoles, why don't we try to come up with a way for us to get into his house and get them back? Or at least bring them a little frozen lettuce," Fink said.

"How are we going to do that?" I asked.

"We could pretend that we're repairmen and we need to get into Mad Dog's room to check all the electrical outlets or something," he said.

"Don't you think he'd recognize us?" I asked.

"Not if we wear hats and false mustaches," Fink answered. "And we could use those old stilts out in your garage to look taller."

I groaned.

"That's never going to work," I said. "Nothing's going to work."

"How do you know if we don't even try?" he asked. "It isn't like you to give up, Nat."

Fink was right. Even though a lot of unlucky things have happened to me in my life, I don't usually give up. Like the time I dropped my keys down the sewer grate. I must have spent three solid hours with a fishing pole and a magnet trying to hook them. And I did eventually manage to pull them out, along with a buck and a half worth of change and a Washington State license plate from 1959.

This was a little different. Actually, this was a lot different. But if Fink thought there was some way to save my tadpoles from starving or maybe even get them back, I wasn't about to give up.

"I don't think fake mustaches and hats will work, but what about making a periscope so we can look in Mad Dog's window and check on the tadpoles without him being able to see us?" I said.

"Now you're talking!" said Fink.

An hour later, we had unwound five rolls of paper towels and used up a whole roll of tape trying to attach some broken pieces of mirror to a bunch of empty cardboard tubes.

"Okay, I think maybe I got it this time," Fink said, holding out the wobbly contraption we'd made, "Look in it now and tell me what you see."

I looked through the end of the cardboard tube and heaved a sigh.

"All I see is my own eye again," I said. "Face it, Fink, this is not going to work."

"You're right," said Fink, taking the periscope from me and looking through it one last time for himself before bending it in half and shoving it into the wastebasket, "But at least it got your mind off those tadpoles for a little while."

"I'm thirsty," I said. "Want some juice?"

As we came into the kitchen, the phone started to ring. I thought maybe it was my mom calling from her ortho emergency, but it turned out to be Jessie.

"What do you want?" I asked.

"I'm calling to remind you that the meeting is at your house tomorrow at four o'clock," she said.

To tell you the truth, I'd been so busy worrying about my kidnapped tadpoles, I'd completely forgotten about the meeting.

"Whatever," I said. I was too tired to even argue.

"What's the matter with you? You sound weird," Jessie said. "You're going to be there for the meeting, aren't you?"

Fink was standing right next to me.

"Is that Jessie?" he asked.

I nodded.

"Give me the phone," he said, holding out his hand for it.

Don't even bother to say it, I know I should have known better, but I handed him the phone.

"Listen, Jessie," Fink said. "You have to leave Nat alone because he's sick. Really sick. He has this rare disease that will paralyze him if he doesn't get some tadpoles soon —"

I jumped up, grabbed the phone away from Fink,

95

and slammed it down on the hook before he could completely ruin what little was left of my doomed life.

"You have to stop telling people that stupid story," I yelled. "You're only going to make things worse. Nobody's going to believe it anyway, can't you see that?"

"Hey, what are you yelling at me for? I'm only trying to help you," Fink said. "I thought maybe if Jessie felt sorry for you, she'd call off the meeting."

"If you really want to help me, why don't you just go home now and leave me alone?" I yelled.

"Fine with me. I don't need to hang around you and your lousy bad luck anymore anyway," Fink said.

"You know something, I used to think I was born with this bad luck," I said as I followed him out to the door. "But you know, maybe that's not it at all. Maybe it's you. Maybe you're the one who makes all this bad stuff happen."

"Are you blaming your bad luck on *me*?" Fink asked, turning around to face me. His cheeks always turn pink when he gets mad, and this time they were really pink.

"You were there when Mad Dog started hating me, and you were there when Jessie and Marla started making fun of me. And if I hadn't been wasting my time waiting in line with you at the Bee Hive after school today, maybe I would have gotten home in time to save my tadpoles from being kidnapped," I said.

I guess Fink was pretty mad after that because he slammed the door really hard when he left.

"Great," I said. "Now everybody hates me."

CHAPTER ELEVEN

I was upstairs brushing my teeth when I heard my mom finally come home. When I was little, my mom had been the one I went to when things went wrong. She was the one who put on Band-Aids, and took out splinters, and always knew the right thing to say to make me feel better. I thought about running down and telling her about Mad Dog, and the tadpoles, and Jessie, and everything. Maybe if I begged she would be willing to let me switch to a new school or something. But I knew if I asked her, she'd probably get all freaked out about it, and that was about the last thing I needed right now — a freaked-out mom. Especially mine. I reminded myself of Fink's powwow experience and promised myself that no matter what, I would not tell my mother what was going on.

I heard her banging dishes around down in the kitchen, and the beep of the microwave as she heated up her own plate of macaroni and cheese.

"Natty?" she called up to me. "You up there?"

"Yeah, Mom," I yelled back down. "I'm here."

"Don't be a stranger, honey, come down and say hi," she called.

I looked at myself in the hall mirror as I passed it on my way downstairs. Same old face. Same old blue eyes and dirty blond hair. It seemed weird that I could look like my normal self when my whole life was so totally messed up.

I went in the kitchen and sat down across from my mom at the table.

"So, what was your ortho emergency?" I asked.

"There were two actually. That's why I'm so late," she said. "I have a patient who didn't wear his rubber bands all month. The little dickens knew I was going to notice at his checkup. So to try to make up for it fast, he put on twenty rubber bands at the same time and wore them all day. He ended up getting a cramp in his jaw so bad, he couldn't talk or eat. His mother called the office and demanded I make a house call to come see her son and remove his braces immediately. She told me if I didn't do what she wanted, she'd have her husband sue me. Can you believe that? She actually threatened to sue me!"

"Was this kid's last name Dundee, by any chance?" I asked.

"Yes. Charlie Dundee," she said. "How on earth did you know that?"

"His sister, Marla, is in my class," I said. "She threatens to sue Fink and me all the time. I guess it runs in the family."

"Does she have red hair?" my mother asked. "I think I might have seen her peeking around the corner tonight when I was dealing with Charlie. She's cute."

"No she's not!" I said.

"I didn't realize she was in your class," said my mom. "I can't seem to keep track anymore. I see so many kids every day, I guess they just kind of blend together into one big mass of crooked teeth and broken brackets after a while."

I sat with my mom while she finished her dinner. She told me it took more than an hour to calm Mrs. Dundee down and convince Charlie that the rubber bands were for his own good, and if he'd just wear a couple of them every night, he'd be out of his braces before he knew it. Actually, she said "in two shakes of a lamb's tail," because unfortunately, as you know, that's the kind of corny thing my mother says.

Listening to her talk got my mind off my problems for a little while, but pretty soon I was back to thinking about Jessie, and Mad Dog, and especially Fink. I felt bad that I'd yelled at him. I didn't blame him for being mad. He didn't deserve to be yelled at that way, no matter what he'd done.

"Nit Nat Patty Whack," my mother said (Fink and I are not the only ones who give people nicknames), "is everything okay? You seem a little distracted or something. Anything going on at school I should know about?"

You mean anything like a big club-armed bully

with catcher's-mitt hands hating my guts for no good reason and stealing my tadpoles so he could take them home and eat them, for instance? Or did you mean had I yelled at the only real friend I had in the world when all he was trying to do was help me?

"Not really," I said. "Nothing unusual going on. Nope."

I kissed my mom good night and went upstairs to take a long hot shower. Afterward, I put on a couple of layers of Manly Mint, just in case. Back in my room, I remembered something I'd been meaning to do all day. I pulled the big dictionary off the shelf and turned to the D's.

D-e-f—*defeat, defect, defend,* there it was, *defenestration* — "*a throwing of a person or thing out of a window.*" Ha-ha. Very funny, Jessie.

My mom stuck her head in the door after I'd already turned out the light.

"You asleep, Nit Nat?" she asked.

"Not yet," I said.

"I forgot to ask you, did you get your tadpoles today?" she asked me.

"No," I said. "I didn't get them."

It was true. They'd come, but I hadn't gotten them.

"Maybe tomorrow," she said.

I knew I wouldn't get them. Not tomorrow. Not the next day. Not ever. I didn't want to talk about it, so I changed the subject.

"I forgot to ask you what the second emergency was, Mom. You said you had two," I said.

"Oh, it's a curious one. I have this new patient, and he has a phobia," she said.

"What's that?" I asked.

"A fear of something," she explained. "Like people who are afraid of being in small spaces have what's called *claustrophobia*. *Hydrophobia* is a fear of the water. There are hundreds of them."

"What's this kid afraid of?" I asked.

"Me," she said.

My mother is about the most unscary person in the world. She uses corny expressions and she doesn't have cookies in the house, but she's really friendly and she's got a very pretty face, too.

"Why's he afraid of you?" I asked.

"Because he's afraid of dentists. His mother says he hasn't had his teeth cleaned in years because he totally falls apart every time she tries to take him there. You wouldn't know it to look at him. He's a great big, tough-looking kid, but first he cried, and then he fainted in my office this afternoon. I ended up going out to his home tonight to do the initial examination there, where at least he could be in familiar surroundings. Poor Douglas. He really needs braces, not to mention a good cleaning, but I'm not sure he's going to be able to handle it."

"Douglas?" I said as I pushed myself up on one elbow and looked at my mother framed in the yellow light of the open doorway.

"Yes. Douglas Ditmeyer. Do you know him, honey?"

CHAPTER TWELVE

I was beginning to worry about how many weird dreams I was having. It seemed like all day long, embarrassing or confusing or upsetting things kept happening to me, and then the minute I closed my eyes, embarrassing, confusing, and upsetting things started happening to me in my sleep, too. One minute it was you-know-who in the poofy wedding dress, then Vasco da Gama, and then the night my mother told me about Mad Dog fainting in her office, I had a dream that *he* was running around in the poofy wedding gown. Talk about scary.

The next morning, I waited out in front of Fink's house at the usual time so we could walk to school together. I wasn't going to tell him about the dream I'd had the night before, but I was dying to tell him that I'd found out that Mad Dog was afraid of my mother. I knew he was going to love it. I waited and waited, but Fink didn't come out. I figured maybe he was sick, so I walked up to his front door and rang the bell.

"Hi, Mrs. Fink, is Boyd sick today?" I asked when Fink's mom opened the door in her bathrobe.

"Oh, hello, Nat. No, Boyd's fine, but he's left already. He said he had to go early for some sort of a meeting this morning," she said. "Didn't he tell you about it? I thought you two told each other everything."

A meeting? What kind of meeting could Fink have had that he wouldn't have told me about? All of a sudden, I understood. Fink hadn't gone to a meeting. He'd just made up that excuse so he wouldn't have to walk to school with me. He was still mad about the night before. Mrs. Fink was right. Except for my dreams, Fink and I do tell each other everything. But standing there on Fink's porch that morning, I wondered if I'd blown it and that wasn't how things were going to be anymore. Maybe Fink didn't even want to be friends with me.

I told Mrs. Fink I must have gotten mixed up and forgotten about his meeting, and then I left and walked to school by myself. Other than when one of us had been sick, I hadn't walked to school alone since Fink and I met all the way back in first grade. I hated it.

On the way, I thought about what I'd said to him about him bringing me bad luck. I knew it wasn't true. Fink wasn't bad for me. He was good for me. When I was bummed out, like I'd been the night before, who was the one patting me on the back, putting up with all my complaining, and telling me everything was going to be okay? Fink. The more I thought about it, the faster I walked. I wanted to get to school and find him so I could tell him I was sorry I'd yelled at him and that I had been totally wrong about everything. I just hoped he would forgive me.

When I got to school, I looked around for Fink out in the yard, but he was nowhere in sight. Henry

Rodnower, a kid from my class, was locking up his bike in the bike racks as I walked toward the entrance of the school.

"Hey, Henry," I said, "you haven't seen Fink anywhere, have you?"

Henry shook his head. Just then, Marla and Jessie showed up. They were wearing matching outfits, of course — pink shirts with fringe on the sleeves and stupid-looking blue pants with butterflies on them. Even though I thought they looked ridiculous dressed alike like that, seeing them together, giggling and clapping hands with each other, reminded me of what I was missing — Fink. When the Red Devils caught sight of me, they immediately started whispering. Finally, Jessie walked over to where I was standing and stopped a few feet away.

"It's not catching, is it?" she said.

"What?" I said.

"Your disgusting disease," she said.

"I don't have any disease," I told her. "I'm fine."

Marla joined us, but like Jessie, she didn't come too close.

"My mother told me that sometimes when people are sick, they don't smell good. Maybe that's the reason you stink, Nat," Marla said.

I wanted to say, "Oh, yeah? Well, my mother told me your little brother is an idiot!" even though I knew what she'd actually said was that he was a little dickens. But I didn't say anything at all. Somehow, without Fink there beside me, I didn't have the nerve to fight back.

The bell rang, and we went inside. When we got to the classroom, Fink's seat was empty. Where was he? He wasn't at home, he wasn't on the playground, and he wasn't at school. Something occurred to me that really got me worried. Maybe Fink had run away. Maybe I'd made him feel so bad, he'd gone off somewhere by himself. What if something happened to him? What if he got hurt? I would never forgive myself.

When Mrs. West called attendance and Fink didn't answer, she asked me where he was.

"Is Mr. Fink ill this morning, Mr. Boyd?"

"I don't think so," I said.

"Then where is he?" she asked.

I shrugged.

"I'm not really sure," I said.

Mrs. West looked surprised. She knows how close Fink and I are. She looked a little worried then, too. Suddenly, Marla spoke up.

"I heard that Nat is sick, Mrs. West, and that maybe what he has is catching and even possibly fatal. He and Boyd are together all the time. I even saw them drink out of the same glass once. I'll bet Nat made Boyd sick, too, and he just doesn't want to admit it," she said. "If he makes me sick, I think I should warn you that my father will definitely sue the school —"

"I'm not sick," said a familiar voice from the back of the class.

It was Fink! He was all right! Well, except for one thing — he was covered with mud. A total mess.

"I'm glad you could join us, Mr. Fink," said Mrs. West. "Now that you're here, I think it might be best for you to go to the lavatory and clean yourself up."

"Can I help him?" I asked. "Please?"

Sometimes Mrs. West isn't so bad. I think she

could tell that I needed to talk to Fink, and she let me go with him.

"No monkey business, you two," she said.

I practically ran across the room to where Fink was standing, dripping water and mud on the floor. I wanted to hug him, I was so happy to see him, but I knew everybody was watching us, and I didn't want to embarrass him.

"I'm really sorry," I said as soon as we got out in the hall. "I didn't mean anything I said last night."

"I'm the one who should be sorry," he said.

"For what? All you did was try to help me. First, you called Mad Dog for me, and then you did those imitations to distract Jessie, and then —"

"Yeah, I know, but it really was my fault you weren't home in time to save your tadpoles from Mad Dog," he said as we walked into the boys' bathroom. "I tried to get some more for you this morning to make up for everything, down at Miller's Swamp. That's how I got so muddy."

"You went to Miller's Swamp?" I said. I couldn't believe he'd done that for me. Miller's Swamp is two miles from our neighborhood. No wonder he'd left home early that morning. How many kids had a best friend who would do something like that for them?

"I thought I saw one, but when I tried to catch it, I slipped and fell in," Fink said as he turned on the water and reached for the soap.

"I just want you to know, I feel really lucky right now," I said.

I knew it was kind of a sappy thing to say, but I didn't care. I meant it. I felt really lucky to have a friend like Fink.

"Uh, did you just say you feel lucky, Nat-o? Because if you're feeling lucky, how come your knee is itching?" asked Fink nervously.

I hadn't noticed it, but Fink was right. I was scratching again.

Just then, the door burst open and Mad Dog came barging into the bathroom. He looked madder and meaner than ever.

"I know what you're doing in here, you little rat," he hissed at me. "You're blabbing to your buddy, aren't you? You know what I do to blabbermouths?"

I had a feeling I did know. Mad Dog grabbed me and pushed me up against the wall.

"I warned you," he said. "I told you not to tell anybody."

"I didn't tell anybody," I said.

"I'm not falling for that," Mad Dog said, then he let go of me, grabbed Fink and pushed him up against the wall. "I know you know. He tells you everything, doesn't he?"

"Look, I know about the tadpoles, if that's what you mean, but I swear Nat and I didn't tell anybody you took them."

"What are you talking about? I didn't take any stinking tadpoles," said Mad Dog. He took his hands off Fink and then looked down at them. They were all muddy from Fink's clothes.

"If you didn't steal them," said Fink, "then what was in the box you took off Nat's porch yesterday? The porch you spit on, in case you think nobody was watching."

I couldn't believe Fink was talking to him that way. Even though I knew about Mad Dog's phobia, he was still pretty scary up close. He was huge. And he was mad.

"I was on the porch, but I'm telling you, I didn't take any stinking tadpoles," he said again.

"Wait," I said. I'd just figured something out. I don't know why I hadn't realized it earlier, but I'd seen those white boxes a million times before. My mom gives them to all her new patients. They have toothbrushes, floss, and information about taking care of your braces in them. Welcome kits, she calls them.

"He didn't take the tadpoles," I said. "Mad Dog is innocent."

"He is?" said Fink. "Then what was in the box?"

Mad Dog looked at his muddy hands, then he walked over to me and wiped them on the front of my shirt.

"If you say one word about anything, I'll cream you," he said. I thought maybe he was going to punch me then, but instead he started to walk away.

I swallowed hard and then called after him.

"Wait," I said, "I'm sorry I accused you of stealing

my tadpoles, Mad Dog, but I can't do what you asked me to do. I can't and I won't. Fink and I tell each other everything. Go ahead and cream me if you want, but I'm not going to keep a secret from my best friend."

Fink looked at me and his mouth fell open. Then he smiled a big wide smile.

"Cool," he said.

Mad Dog seemed surprised. I guess he'd never run into anybody who would rather get pounded than do something to mess up a friendship.

"I'll make a deal with you," I said. "I'm going to tell Fink your secret, but I promise I won't tell anybody else and neither will he, as long as you hold up your end of the bargain," I said.

"What bargain?" he growled.

I told him what I had in mind. He wasn't too happy about it, but in the end, Mad Dog agreed to the deal. We even shook on it. His hands are actually not as big as catcher's mitts — but almost.

CHAPTER THIRTEEN

That afternoon after school, we had a meeting of the Vasco da Gama group at four o'clock at my house. Jessie was the last to arrive. Fink let her in. I think she was pretty surprised to find Mad Dog and me sitting happily together on the couch looking at a book I'd brought home from the library that day.

"See?" I was saying, "this is the picture I was telling you about. That's Vasco da Gama there in the funny hat, and look at all the weapons they've got. Pistols and swords and I forget what those little ones are called —"

"Daggers," said Mad Dog.

"Right, daggers," I said. "There's all kinds of cool

stuff in here about weapons. Like, check out these cannons. They were called bombards and they fired rocks."

Mad Dog just grunted. But it was a friendly grunt, not a mad one.

"You can borrow this book for your part of the report if you want," I told him.

"Thanks," said Mad Dog.

Jessie was staring at us. I could tell she was surprised. I wasn't sweating one little bit. In fact, I was so comfortable, I crossed my arms and put them behind my head just to rub it in a little. I knew Mad Dog wasn't going to do anything bad — we had a deal.

We spent about an hour going over what each of us had done so far on the project. Jessie showed us her map. She'd done a great job coloring it in with markers. I talked about how da Gama had decided he wanted to be a sailor when he was just a little kid, even though his dad had been a soldier. Fink filled us in on some of the problems da Gama had run into.

"There wasn't enough fresh fruit on the ship so all the sailors got sick. Their arms and legs swelled up, and then their teeth fell out. Guess they could have used a dentist on board, huh?"

Mad Dog shot him a look, but he didn't say anything.

Later, when the meeting was over, Mad Dog made his big move.

"Hey, Nat, thanks for inviting me to sleep over on Saturday," he said. "I'm really looking forward to it. Maybe next weekend you can sleep at my house."

He'd memorized word for word what Fink and I came up with for him to say. It didn't sound exactly natural, but it was good enough to fool Jessie, and that's all I cared about. Of course, we weren't really going to have a sleepover. It was just part of the deal Mad Dog and I had made. Fink and I would keep his secret as long as Mad Dog made it seem like we were friends whenever Jessie or Marla was around. Fink had been right. There was no way Jessie could accuse me of being afraid of Mad Dog anymore once she heard about our sleepover plans. She and Marla were going to have to find someone else to pick on for a change.

After Jessie and Mad Dog left, Fink and I went into the kitchen. He'd already asked his mom if it was okay for him to stay for dinner. My mom had said she'd be home by six and that we could order pizza with everything on it as long as I made a green salad and set the table, too. I started washing lettuce at the sink.

"There's something I need to tell you," I said.

"Something bad?" he asked.

"Not exactly," I said.

"Then why do you look so weird?" he asked.

"Probably because I've never told anybody about this thing before," I said. "Not even you."

"I thought we told each other everything," said Fink.

"We do. That's why I'm going to tell you this, even though I don't really want to, because, well, because it's just so embarrassing."

Fink didn't say anything. He just stood there looking at me.

"See, I have these dreams," I began.

Fink laughed, and at first I was kind of upset.

Didn't he understand how hard it was for me to tell him about this? Maybe it was a mistake to confess my secret to him.

"Are they weird, embarrassing, creepy dreams?" he asked.

"Yeah. How did you know?" I said.

"Because I have them, too!" he said.

"Really?" I was amazed.

"Yep. Check this out. The other day after we had that conversation about how dogs don't smile when they're happy, they just wag their tails — remember? — Well, that night I dreamed it was my birthday, and when my mom brought out the cake with all the candles on it, I jumped up and suddenly, I had this big old furry tail sticking right out the back of my pants, and I started wagging it right in front of everybody," he said.

For the second time that day, I felt like hugging Fink.

"That's so weird!"

"So tell me one of yours," he said.

"Okay. I dreamed about Jessie in a poofy wedding

gown. She came over to me and —" I whispered the rest of it in Fink's ear because it was just too embarrassing to say out loud.

Fink was howling.

"That's not a dream, that's a nightmare!" he cried.

I was glad I'd told him. It felt good not to be keeping a secret from him anymore.

"You promise not to tell anyone?" Fink said. "You know, about the tail?"

"Promise," I said.

We spit on our palms and rubbed them together to cement the oath. Then I picked up the salad bowl and a handful of silverware and headed out to the dining room to set the table.

"Don't worry, Fink," I told him. "My mom won't make you eat any salad tonight. She goes easy on company."

"How long till the pizza gets here?" asked Fink. "I'm kind of hungry. Are you sure there isn't a stash of cookies hidden in here someplace?" Fink asked, heading back toward the kitchen.

"Positive," I said.

"Don't you have anything to snack on?" he asked, pulling out a jar of wheat germ and looking at it unhappily.

"Sure. A or B? You want a carrot or a health food bar?"

"Hey, no fair. I gave you an extra choice last time we played. You gotta do that, too," Fink said.

"Okay, fine. You want some worms?" I asked.

"I do, if they're gummy worms!" he said.

I was carrying three plates out to the dining room table when the doorbell rang.

"Pizza!" Fink cried.

"There's no way it could get here that fast. I just ordered it a second ago," I said. "Somebody probably forgot something at the meeting." I set down the stack of plates and went to answer the door.

It wasn't Jessie or Mad Dog, though. It was the mailman. He was holding a small box.

"Special delivery for Nathaniel Boyd," he said.

"Hey, Fink!" I called out to the kitchen. "Grab that bag of frozen lettuce out of the freezer, will you? We've got company for dinner!"

NAT'S MOM'S CORNY EXPRESSIONS

Do you remember reading these expressions?
Can you finish them? Look back through the book.
When you find the saying, fill in the blank lines.
Jot down the page number, too!

His _____ was worse than his _____. _____

Adding _____ to the _____. _____

Cool as a _____. _____

Like there was no _____. _____

Hook, line, and _____. _____

Killing two _____ with _____ stone. _____

In two _____ of a lamb's _____. _____

ABOUT THE AUTHOR

Sarah Weeks has written numerous picture books and novels, including *Mrs. McNosh Hangs up Her Wash; Two Eggs, Please; Follow the Moon;* and the popular *Regular Guy* series for middle-grade readers. *My Guy,* the third in that series, is currently in production at Disney for a feature-length, live-action film.

Ms. Weeks is a singer/songwriter as well as an author. Many of her books, such as *Angel Face, Crocodile Smile,* and *Without You,* include CDs of her original songs. She visits many schools and libraries throughout the country every year, speaking at assemblies and serving as author-in-residence. She lives in New York City with her two teenage sons.